Edward Lear

Illustrations copyright © Owen Wood, 1978

Published in 1979 by the Viking Press
625 Madison Avenue, New York, N.Y. 10022

First published in Great Britain in 1978 by
André Deutsch Limited
105 Great Russell Street London WC1
in association with
HEINRICH HANAU PUBLICATIONS

ISBN 0-670-53314-9

Printed in England by
Sackville Press Billericay Ltd

Edward Lear

The Owl & the Pussy-Cat & Other Nonsense

Illustrated by

A STUDIO BOOK

THE VIKING PRESS · NEW YORK

For Clare, Robert & James

The Owl
& the
Pussy-Cat

The Owl and the Pussy-Cat went to sea
In a beautiful pea-green boat,

They took some honey, and plenty of money,
Wrapped up in a five-pound note.

The Owl looked up to the stars above,
    And sang to a small guitar,
"O lovely Pussy! O Pussy, my love,
"What a beautiful Pussy you are,
          "You are,
          "You are!
"What a beautiful Pussy you are!"

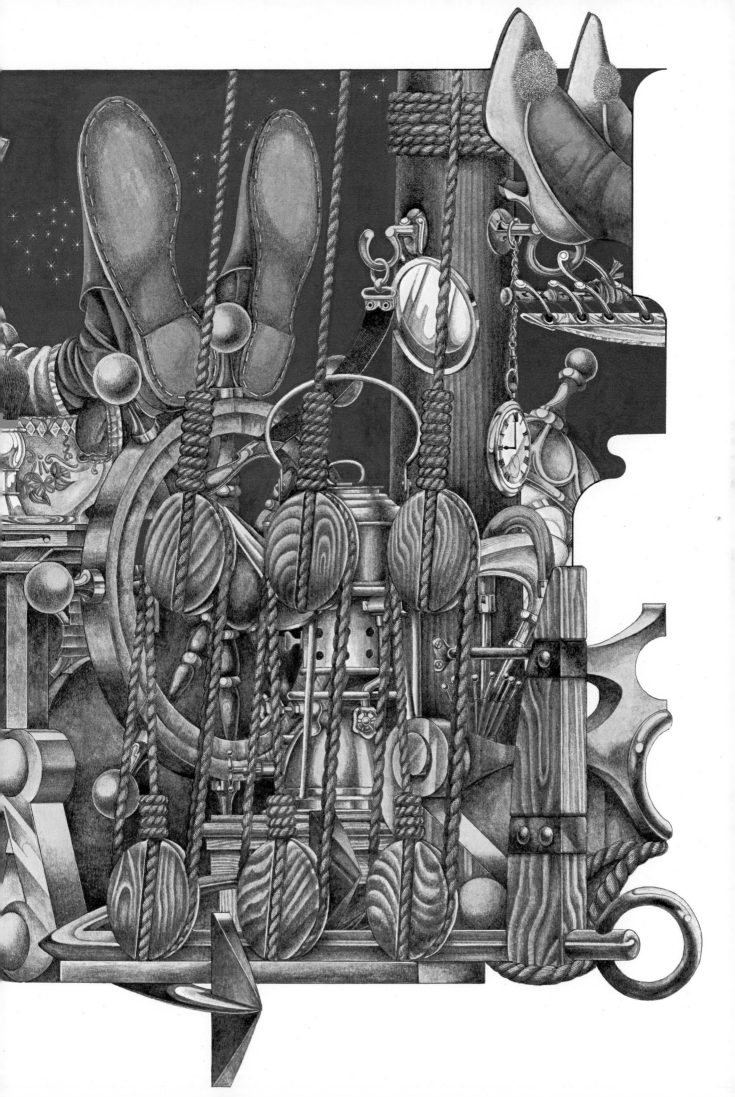

Pussy said to the Owl, "You elegant fowl!
"How charmingly sweet you sing!
"O let us be married! too long we have tarried:
"But what shall we do for a ring?"

They sailed away for a year and a day,
To the land where the Bong-tree grows,

And there in a wood a Piggy-wig stood,
With a ring at the end of his nose,
His nose,
His nose,
With a ring at the end of his nose.

"Dear Pig, are you willing to sell for one shilling
"Your ring?" Said the Piggy, "I will."

*So they took it away, and were married next day
By the Turkey who lives on the hill.*

They dined on mince, and slices of quince,
Which they ate with a runcible spoon;

And hand in hand, on the edge of the sand,
They danced by the light of the moon,
The moon,
The moon,
They danced by the light of the moon.

& Other Nonsense

There was an Old Man, who when little
Fell casually into a Kettle;
But, growing too stout,
He could never get out,
So he passed all his life in that Kettle.

There was an Old Man of the Hague,
Whose ideas were excessively vague;
He built a balloon
To examine the moon,
That deluded Old Man of the Hague.

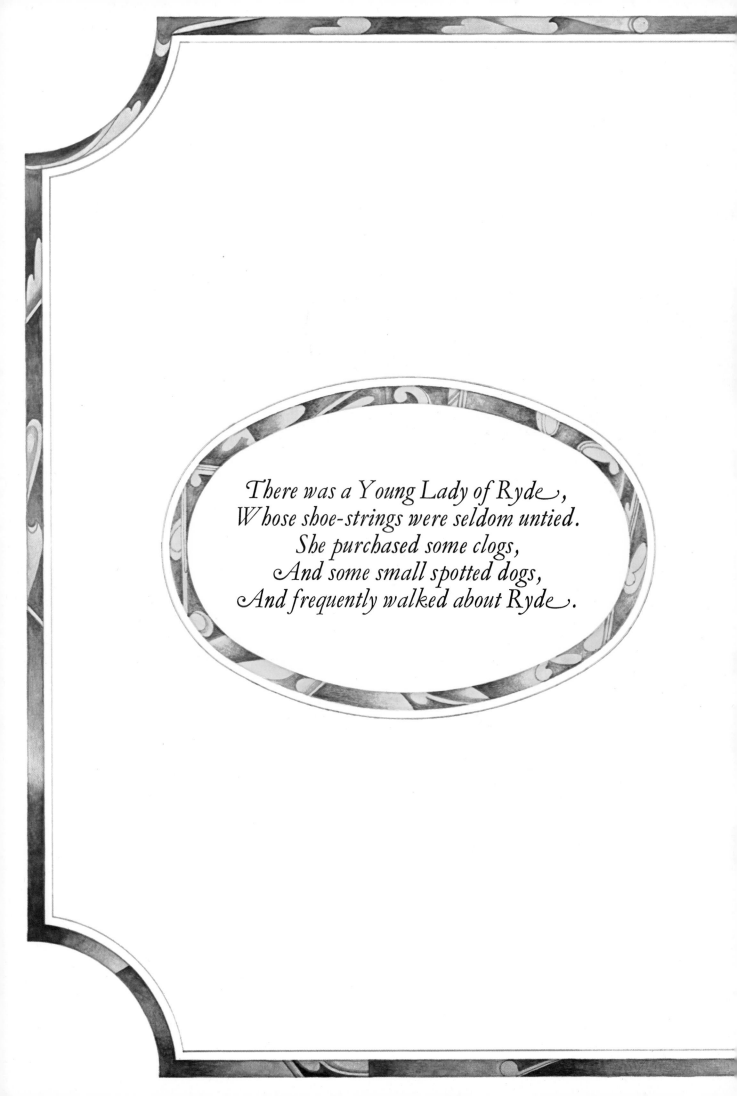

There was a Young Lady of Ryde,
Whose shoe-strings were seldom untied.
She purchased some clogs,
And some small spotted dogs,
And frequently walked about Ryde.

There was an Old Man of Dunluce,
Who went out to sea on a Goose;
When he'd gone out a mile,
He observ'd with a smile,
"It is time to return to Dunluce."

There was an Old Man of Blackheath,
Whose head was adorned with a Wreath,
Of lobsters and spice,
Pickled onions and mice,
That uncommon Old Man of Blackheath.

There was a Young Lady of Welling,
Whose praise all the world was a-telling;
She played on a harp,
And caught several carp,
That accomplished Young Lady of Welling.

There was an Old Man in a tree,
Who was horribly bored by a bee;
When they said, "Does it buzz?"
He replied, "Yes, it does!
It's a regular brute of a bee!"

There was a Young Lady whose bonnet
Came untied when the birds sat upon it;
But she said, "I don't care!
All the birds in the air
Are welcome to sit on my bonnet!"

The End